RUTH DOWLEY

GALA STAR

Illustrated by Strawberrie Donnelly

HODDER
Wayland

an imprint of Hodder Children's Books

Chapter One

I *love* swimming. Our new school was having a Gala Swimming Day the week Mark and I started. I really wanted to be in it.

The new school was a bit scary, though. Not knowing anyone, I mean. It was the middle of term. Everybody would have friends already.

From my bedroom, I'd seen a girl my age swinging on a rope three gardens along. I wondered what she was like. It would be great to have a friend living on the same road.

My heart thumped when Dad woke me for school on Monday.

I have diabetes, so I did a blood sugar count with my testing kit. Then I did my morning insulin injection.

My brother, Mark, crashed out of his room.

"Breakfast," Mum called.

"I have to find my trainers first," Mark shouted. "Want me to go in bare feet?"

I went to look, but Mum called me back. "Eat your cereal, Amy. We don't want you having a hypo."

Mark chucked bags and fallen coats around by the back door.

"Bet they're under the sofa," I said.

They were. Mark shoved in his feet, grinning. It helped that we'd be starting school together.

Doing well at swimming might help, too. I'm pretty fast. I hoped it wasn't too late to be in the gala!

Chapter Two

Miss Patel, my class teacher, asked
a girl called Karla to help me the first
day. She said I'd be in Red, the same
house as Karla.

The bell rang. We lined up for
assembly.

"We're not allowed to talk now,"
Karla bellowed, even though I hadn't
said anything. Everyone giggled.

Then at break, Karla told me where the girls' toilets were so loudly that people turned around. It sounded like I needed to get there quick, or I'd wet myself.

Outside, I unpacked my banana and biscuits. "You don't have to stay with me," I said to Karla.

"I'm supposed to." Karla opened a bar of chocolate. "Want some?"

I shook my head. "No, thanks."

She looked amazed. "Don't you like chocolate?"

"Sometimes."

I was going to say that I can't eat a lot of sweets. My blood sugar gets too high. But I thought she'd blurt it out in her loud-speaker voice. None of the kids knew about my diabetes yet. Everyone in the playground might gawk.

Mark raced past
after a ball.
"That's my
brother," I said.

A boy from our
class got the ball
first. He flicked it
from foot to knee
to forehead.
"Throw it!"
Mark yelled.

The boy whipped it behind him.
"Throw what?" he asked, innocently.
"Come on, Lee!" shouted the
other boys.

Lee headed it at them.
Karla rolled her eyes. "He's such
a goof! He's in Red. He'd better not
lose us points at the swimming gala."
I crossed my fingers that I'd get
a chance to win some.

Karla had brought a packed lunch like me. She steered us to a table. "Hi, Jo-Jo!" she yelled.

A girl looked up. It was the girl from my road!

Chapter Three

"Amy's new in our class," Karla said. "She's in Red. I have to look after her."

Jo-Jo smiled. "Hi! I'm in Yellow. I was away this morning at the dentist's."

I wanted to tell Jo-Jo where I lived, but Karla started talking non-stop...

...that is, until I took out some carrot and celery sticks with my sandwich.

"You like rabbit food?" she asked at the top of her voice.

My face went hot. I'd have to say about watching what I eat with the whole table listening.

But Jo-Jo said, "I've got to eat better if I want to be a good swimmer." She laughed. "I'm getting chubby!"

"You're just about the best swimmer in our class," said Karla.

"Lee's the best," said Jo-Jo.

"You can't count on him. He mucks about."

They talked about the gala. I was all ears.

"We'll probably practise the relays in swimming tomorrow," said Karla.

"I've never done relays in water," I said.

"They're great," said Jo-Jo. "But I would think that. I'm mad on swimming."

I just had time to say, "So am I," before the bell rang.

I hoped to see Jo-Jo walking home. But Miss Patel asked me to wait behind.

"Your mum tells me you're good at looking after your diabetes," she said.

I nodded. "It doesn't stop me doing anything. I just need extra snacks at school. Like before sports. So my blood sugar doesn't get too low."

"Right."

I took a big breath and asked her.
"Can I be in the swimming gala?"
"You bet. I'll watch you tomorrow."
Yes!

Chapter Four

Jo-Jo's mouth fell open when she came out of her house in the morning.

"You've moved in here?" she bubbled. "Oh, wow!"

My mum chatted to Jo-Jo's mum as we walked along. I really, really hoped we were going to be friends.

Our class went to the public pool for swimming. I ate a cereal bar and some raisins on the way. I *love* raisins.

The pool looked fabulous. Karla grabbed me and Jo-Jo. "Come on! Ten minutes' free swim to start."

We walked to the edge.

"Here I come!" Lee bombed into the water right in front of us.

Karla screamed. We were soaked.

"Lee-*ee!*" Karla bellowed. "You know you're not supposed to do that."

We jumped in, giggling.

"Swim to the other side," said Jo-Jo.

Jo-Jo and I passed Karla. Jo-Jo went faster. I matched her, stroke for stroke.

We touched the wall dead level and burst out laughing.

"I've got to get fitter," Jo-Jo gasped. "I'm puffed. You're good!"

Miss Patel saw us. She smiled. "We'll put you in the freestyle and the ball relay, Amy."

Freestyle sounded great. But the ball relay turned out to be tricky.

Each team had a big floating ball. The swimmers held it in front of them and kicked their way across the pool.

It bobbed away from me twice. I wished I had more time to practise. What if I made a fool of myself?

Chapter Five

On gala day, I took a sandwich and
a little box of raisins to eat before my
relays. The glucose tablets I always
carry round were in my sweatshirt
pocket, too.

The changing room was packed.

Jo-Jo shouted over the noise. "Want to come and play tomorrow? We've got a rope-swing."

She *did* want to be friends!

"Great!" I said.

The gala started. Everyone got into it, yelling for a house or someone they knew. I was so excited, I forgot to eat my snack. I *never* usually forget.

When Miss Patel threw coins into the pool, I knew it was our year's turn.

The swimmers dived and grabbed coins off the bottom until they ran out of breath. Lee got lots for Red.

He handed them up. Then instead of getting out, he dived again. He stood on his hands in the water.

His feet waved in the air. Everyone laughed, so he got away with it.

My ball relay was called. I was dead worried the ball would bob away.

It did bob away from the girl before me. She swam after it. The Reds groaned.

There had to be a better way to hold it. Wait a minute. There was!

I grabbed the ball and turned on my back. I held it tight against my tummy. My legs kicked full power – straight across.

"Cool idea!" said Jo-Jo, when she handed me my towel.

I didn't put on my sweatshirt, so I *still* forgot to eat my snack.

The freestyle relay was the last race for our year. We were tied with Yellow.

There were four of us in each team. Jo-Jo was going last for Yellow. I was last for Red.

We said, "Have a good one!" at the same time and grinned.

Yellow took the lead. Green dropped back in the next lap. Then Blue.

Lee was in front of me. He took off like a shot. He passed Yellow. A cheer went up.

But almost back, Lee changed his stroke. Holding up his head with a silly smile, he did *the doggy paddle.*

The Reds went screaming mad.
"Don't slow down!"

"You dope, Lee!" Karla bawled.
"STOP MUCKING ABOUT!"

Yellow raced in. Jo-Jo was off.

Finally, Lee touched the end.
I dived.

Chapter Six

Jo-Jo seemed miles ahead. *I swam!* All stops out. I caught up with her just after turning.

Go for it, I told myself. She was going for it, too. It was a great feeling, the two of us doing our best.

I hit the end. A teacher shouted, "Red!"

Clapping and cheering exploded round the pool.

Gasping for breath, Jo-Jo and I went to our seats, arms round each other. Kids patted me on the back.

Karla shouted, "Mega-brilliant! Gala Star!" For once, I loved her loud voice.

I felt very tired as I watched Mark
in the diving. I got more and more
sweaty.

"That's your brother, isn't it?" asked
Jo-Jo.

I couldn't answer. She went blurry.
Something weird was happening.

"Wake up, Amy!" bellowed Karla. "You look spaced-out."

She wobbled. So did the other kids. So did the teachers and the walls. It was like I was back in the pool. Under water!

I started shaking. Oh, no, *no*,
I thought. *I'm having a hypo.*

A blur of Mark rushed towards me.

"Where are your glucose tablets?"
He yanked them out of my sweatshirt
pocket and tore open the packet.
"Quick! Eat some!"

"What's wrong?" asked everyone.

"She's got diabetes. Her blood sugar's gone too low. She needs to get it level again or she might pass out."

"Oh, *Amy!*" gasped Jo-Jo. "Why didn't you tell us?"

Karla raced to Miss Patel. She came and knelt beside Mark.

I sucked a glucose tablet, then another. By the third one, the wobbling stopped. I was back on dry land.

Re-lief!

"I forgot my snack," I explained. "I'll be OK if I eat it now."

Jo-Jo's arm went round me as I started on my sandwich and raisins.

Chapter Seven

Next day in class, the other kids asked lots of questions. "Is diabetes catching?" (No.) "Does it hurt to give yourself injections?" (Not much.)

Miss Patel said I might need to eat snacks during lessons.

Lee waved his hand in the air, grinning. "Are snacks the *raisin* you swim fast?"

Everybody laughed.

"No, you doggy paddler!" bellowed Karla. "*She* goes for it!"

I was glad everyone knew about my diabetes now. On the way home, Jo-Jo said if I forget my snack before sports again, she'll remind me.

We had a great time together on her rope-swing. I think Jo-Jo's going to be my best friend ever.

Look out for these other titles in the Shooting Stars range:

Top Biker by Ruth Dowley
Steve has trouble walking. So when he learns to ride a bike with the help of his best mates, Ravi and Kipper, everyone's amazed. Steve would be having the time of his life, if it wasn't for the school bully, Dan Atkins.

The Castle Awakes by Paeony Lewis
The prince wakes Sleeping Beauty with a kiss and there's a royal wedding to plan. But the prince is terrified of spiders, and after a hundred years, there are a lot of spiders to deal with. Worse still, the cunning creepy-crawlies want to keep the castle for themselves. Will the prince and Sleeping Beauty live happily ever after?

You can buy all these books from your local bookseller, or order them direct from the publisher. For more information about Shooting Stars, write to: *The Sales Department, Hodder Children's Books, a division of Hodder Headline Limited, 338 Euston Road, London NW1 3BH.*